GW01157571

# GET TO YOUR STARTING POINT

to fulfill your potential.

EDWARD STEEP

authorHOUSE®

*AuthorHouse™ UK*
*1663 Liberty Drive*
*Bloomington, IN 47403 USA*
*www.authorhouse.co.uk*
*Phone: UK TFN: 0800 0148641 (Toll Free inside the UK)*
*UK Local: (02) 0369 56322 (+44 20 3695 6322 from outside the UK)*



*Published by AuthorHouse 05/30/2024*

*ISBN: 979-8-8230-8793-3 (sc)*
*ISBN: 979-8-8230-8792-6 (hc)*
*ISBN: 979-8-8230-8791-9 (e)*

*Library of Congress Control Number: 2024910747*

*Print information available on the last page.*



*This book is printed on acid-free paper.*

# CONTENTS

# A NOTE FROM THE AUTHOR

*This Book is a work of fiction and bends creditability and truth in order to entertain. If any Reader takes offence from these words I immediately apologise as that was certainly not my intention. I believe in a higher being but do not believe in religious creeds as I make my own standards and treat all humans equally, with kindness and wisdom within my personal abilities. All books of faith have value and should be used as tools positively, not prescriptively, as all people have different levels of ability to understand and show/demonstrate their faith "as they see it". None of us are perfect. And any reference to actual persons, living or dead, or to actual events or locales is entirely coincidental.*

**Moving on.... A few notes on Earthquakes & Climate Change may help some Readers......**

**Google.com says:- <u>Earthquakes</u> are vibrations caused by rocks breaking under stress against an underground surface called a fault plane whereas a <u>Tremor</u> is an involuntary movement of the earth surface caused by stress in the underground rocks. They are both signs of seismic movement.**

**<u>People in the UK</u> are highly unlikely to suffer earthquake problems/damage. However, history tells us UK Housing experiences earthquakes up to about 4.5 magnitude (Richter scale is of 1 – 10 but could be higher in theory but also note that a mag 5 is ten times more powerful than a mag 4 etc...) roughly once every 2 years or so; this magnitude is too small to be felt and they are localised.**

**Building Regulations also require Homes to be built to withstand WIND SPEEDS from 85mph (37m/sec) in the South to over 120mph (54m/sec) in the far North. Such high winds only occur once in about every 50 years.**

**Probably the best type of Home Construction type to withstand such forces is REINFORCED CONCRETE FRAME. Obviously the greater the density of the construction type (like reinforced concrete) the better (plus the more robust its fixings) the more the outside frame will withstand wind and other forces (subject to exposure and slope index readings etc....).**

**The Author, a retired Chartered Surveyor, has recorded statistics from the WWW, such as weather patterns heating up slowly and globally (mainly due to *increases in greenhouses gases)* plus other data. The consequence is well known in that the seasons are changing for plants and animals. Between 1900 and 2019 average global sea**

level rose by 0.21m (mainly due to resultant sea ice melt). This affects us all.

## But what does climate change mean?

Short-wave radiation (heat from the sun is allowed through the atmosphere and to heat the Earth's surface. The Earth then gives off more heat (Long-wave radiation). This heat is trapped by *greenhouse* gases (e.g. methane, carbon dioxide and nitrous oxide) which radiate the heat back towards Earth thus again heating up the Earth. A repeating circular process of doom called *Global Warming.* The human activities that HELP this process can be codified as:-

- Burning fossil fuels (more carbon dioxide)
- Deforestation (more carbon dioxide)
- Dumping waste in landfill (producing methane)

- **Agriculture (eg: release of nitrogen oxides via Cow/ Animal waste)**
- **Natural processes (eg: multiple small scales)**

**RESULTS from these effects COULD INCLUDE……**

1. **Rise in sea levels (particularly East Coast of England and 80 million affected worldwide).**
2. **Drought and Flooding (changes in coastlines can be expected).**
3. **Much increased demand for Water in Hotter Summers.**
4. **Industry may be impacted (eg: Scottish Ski Resorts due to lack of snow?).**
5. **Tropical Storms worsen.**
6. **Species may become extinct eg: especially in the Artic.**
7. **Diseases such as Malaria increase - perhaps 280 million people affected worldwide.**

8. **Changes in frequency of Earthquakes/Tremors/ Volcanoes/Storms.**
9. **UK weather becomes more extreme - Insurance problematic? - Hardship cases increase? Damage widespread.**

**So you now know the nasties that could happen, in theory, but most probably will not occur.**

# BACK-STORY COMMENTS

After a severe sand storm Scientists/Experts are exploring a newly revealed cave deep into the Holyland. Excitement was high as this is exactly the type of place ancient scrolls were often hidden. Even a team of professionals would just about do anything, perhaps even bend a few rules, to achieve a really high grade "find" as the season thus far had been disappointingly flat.

Suddenly the earth moved and the sound of a seeming thousand tornadoes flattened them. The cave air filled with dust and sand as they protected their heads with their arms and hit the deck. An unexpected earth-tremor, by waves, passed through the immediate area. Luckily the cave withstood the shock, albeit battered and beaten.

With fast beating hearts, blooded knuckles and knees the team rose a few minutes later to realise they were as safe as was possible in the circumstances and the real danger had passed them by. Relative silence was golden. Again, out of the blue, deeper inside the cave came an alarmed shout of "**HERE, HERE**." They all ran and looked expecting to see the worse: perhaps injuries, or worse still, deaths. But no.......

Colleagues had unearthed what would best be described as, within a natural rock corner/area, an enclosure that appeared to have been man-made. It was too regular to be natural; perhaps made to hold or surround something of great value and to secrete it for eons?

It had just been damaged by the earth-tremor but it looked like perhaps an unnaturally large traditional amphora enclosed within what was once a wood casing. The area was cleared and we noted it had been within a man-chiselled rock outer jacket, packed inside with a protective layer of smaller rocks and then bound by boulders and then covered by a large but slim roof of a rock set up on four corner pier-stones (that had all been dislodged by the tremor). The wood casing had mainly decayed many, many years ago but traces were detectable/obvious. In other words, all had fallen over to allow viewing of the various layers.

Later what was revealed as remarkable was the amphora had cracked and partially smashed to reveal its contents. What was mainly concealed was a large SCROLL, or perhaps several scrolls mingled together although parts had been exposed and damaged. The tantalising element applied to a brittle part that had been forced out and could now be seen but, as a result, easily read and therefore translated (albeit needing a trained Expert/Professional). The following day saw a translation amounting to the extraordinary statement nobody will ever forget:-

“**Jesus said**: ***My husband and God will not tolerate such actions and words. You must retract your opinions NOW and before the Forum. Females are debarred entry so I must rely upon you to action my teachings.” Speak with***

***my weight and God my father will reward you in Heaven. I will answer questions as and when confronted."***

**MY HUSBAND!** What? This comment would make Jesus a woman.

This is not a new suggestion/assertion but does this new evidence carry sufficient weight to take to General Council? Is it not our duty so to do? Yes. Before we take this further, we must establish if this is the one and only Jesus of Nazareth, the declared son (?) of God? Or not? It appears to be so,….

What must be remembered is that it is now asserted that what we term the bible was not written by a single or several authors, **but by a community of Scribes** but not anyone witnessing the event described above, first hand. The bible is accepted as truth is it not?

Creative back-story events solidify Jesus as a male character and the Bible does not name Authorship as this was an idea from a subsequent era - the later Greek Period. The

Bible tells stories from events recalled many long years, perhaps even decades, after Jesus left this planet so it must be inaccurate to say the least (most stories are records by people who never even met Jesus).

The problem with Authorship is "Did God speak through various people and put words into their heads for them to write the Bible Stories? Or was it truly voluntary and based on first-hand witness statements, ergo real memories?"

ALSO, if you have read what others have said, by whatever method or motivation, about living, religion, God, and holiness etc… and have also seen the good that others have done in the wide world, then it is probable you will follow by that example and lead a straight and narrow course through your own life and act in a similar good way and keep the Ten Commandments etc… Does this make you a holy and reliable witness? Possibly, but not necessarily.

My problem here is why did women in general, from this point onwards, turn away from community leadership plus ruling in general and therefore seek to lead individual Families alone. Did these two functions become mutually exclusive? Raising children, doing the household duties of cooking, cleaning, and organising seasons provisions and clothes such that it became a full-time job. Certainly, somebody had to do these things and a trend had taken hold perhaps before this generation realised these things. However, that decision came at great cost for some people who "had what it would have taken" for such other high-powered roles to be able to be taken in tandem with household roles. Unfortunately for Women, Men stood by and watched with a wicked smile on their faces as they began to take over on a bandwagon of exclusivity and real focus of purpose.

***In many respects this is exactly what happens in many people's lives TODAY as many would say "it is a Mans' world" today (if you let it be so).***

However, back in time, to Jesus's era, Women could have ruled like Queens very easily. So why wasn't the chance taken? (assuming Jesus was a woman and was telling them to lead?).

This is a question that cannot be answered except that could women have loved their flock (children) so well/much that they did not want the distraction that would have come with Ruling a Country or Tribe/the World!. If this was true then they were wise beyond their time: was it that simple and were men that greedy for power that they readily bought into the deception and it was never again discussed?

Behind the scenes Jesus stories were changed by Romans and paid employees of the local Establishment structures that surrounded him as he/she wandered through life.

Perhaps the Establishment welcomed **her** and recorded **him**. A true dichotomy. If only the camera had been invented during the offspring of Gods lifespan on earth. Something that appears to have been a miracle too far.

Jesus was….

- Born of a **woman**.
- Seen first by a **woman** after his resurrection.
- He told a **woman** to tell his disciples that he had risen.
- He never discriminated against **women** (nor was he disparaging).
- From the beginning, Jewish **female disciples**, including Mary Magdalene, Joana, Susanna, and Salome accompanied Jesus during his ministry and supported him out of their own private means.
- Jesus issued miracles **upon women** as easily as on men, and as frequently.

## Turn this situation around……..

The question that reaches my lips was and always is **"Why was not Jesus really a woman as this would have made perfect sense?"**

Why? I hear you ask. The end of Jesus on earth was caused by him/her taking a step too far and not repenting to those Authorities. Result? Crucifixion (plus an assortment of whip, nailing and sword wounds) as his/her Capital Punishment. He died and ascended to Heaven to be with his Father after leaving examples for all of us to follow for evermore unless/until he intervenes again by way of direct personal action.

I ask myself "would a woman have been more empathic and taken a less confrontational route to bring society round to her way of thinking and worshipping at all levels locally, regionally and on a world scale. Now quite as obviously I know nothing about women and their ability to travel the world at that time etc… so please do not shoot me down. But do remember we are talking about the son (or should I say daughter) of God who could perform or create miracles!

- Men fought wars and spent long periods “in the fields” growing foodstuffs (**away from the actual home unit**).
- Women often **gathered** to talk (whilst the men were away from the home unit).

**My proposition is that Jesus could have been much more efficient if he went to female groupings day-to-day to spread his/her teachings**. OK, convince the Husband and he “told” his wife– this might have been the formulae Jesus was working to BUT for each COUPLE he could convert he could have multiplied that by a higher factor if he had gone down the female strain daily. The female social model multiplied at a faster and higher rate than the male social factor. Men did not always talk convincingly, or at all, to their partners!

**I cannot say how far, or how much this delayed his Grand Plan on Earth, but do believe it slowed his teachings**

**considerably and possibility altered the quality of the echo effect of his word as it rippled through society**.

Men were entrenched in their own chosen religious sect and women were exposed less than men to the word of God through Jesus making and taking his word less efficiently to women than to men. I hope you followed this logic.

I am questioning the wisdom of God in spreading his wisdom through Jesus. This projected pathway for his Son resulted in a Crucifixion death. Who am I to say this was misguided; me a mere nobody who is most probably missing the point. As a father I could not place my own son in such a position so this probably blinds me (but surely God would have known what outcome was in store for his only son). Also, who am I to question the wisdom of a higher being? I am merely a logical bystander from their future using hindsight as I see it.

One problem with the above INTRO statements is the thought "**WHAT CAUSED THE MALE STORIES OF**

**JESUS TO BE WRITTEN IN THE FIRST PLACE?"** I believe the answer is ***The Disciples*** *and those who they influenced by verbal testament through the ages.*

Were women "in decline" so deeply that lies had to be delivered on a large scale to begin a deluge to make things begin to turn around? Scriptures bought this "change" and the rest is written as history. We perpetuate that history by taking Scrolls from the sand and add many years to those what? Lies? And so it goes on….. We are still discussing (the place of) women in society here in the 21st Century as their place/role is determined by mainly men and written history (which is slowly changing).

Indeed, how do we reconcile the terms **MOTHER EARTH** / **MOTHER NATURE**? One theory put forward runs as follows:-

Perhaps it all started when Christianity became the State Religion of the Roman Empire in 313AD and things changed. Much evidence suggests that the **female line was**

**the previously the stronger sex and had dominated earth for centuries;** for example, as per the writings of Paul in the New Testament.

**The catalyst of change seems to have been Constantine becoming Roman Emperor and Christianity attaining Civil Power** – the boys were back and were not going to give up their power base. Indeed, newly gained power was the reason they used to justify violence to stay in power; all sorts of things stem from this period (with some variations) ---- ***past female power evidence was obliterated*** by plays acted by Males playing female parts, goddesses raped or overthrown, women's right to sexuality was strictly controlled and sexual pleasure was redefined as sinful and placed in the control of the Father or Husband. Also, Female circumcision was used to protect virginity but was performed (in a) highly barbaric and painful manner.

**All this was to grant the Male Sex true power and influence. And it worked.**

The result was that Men started to Rule. Mainly. Women were reduced to Sex Partners and Influencer status or an ordinary "nothing" until time began to slowly change things for the better.

**What a backdrop! This Book *Story* begins below…in today's timeframe….*an observation on two individuals who have a special path to follow if they accept/recognise the challenge.***

# GET TO YOUR STARTING POINT

to fulfill your potential.

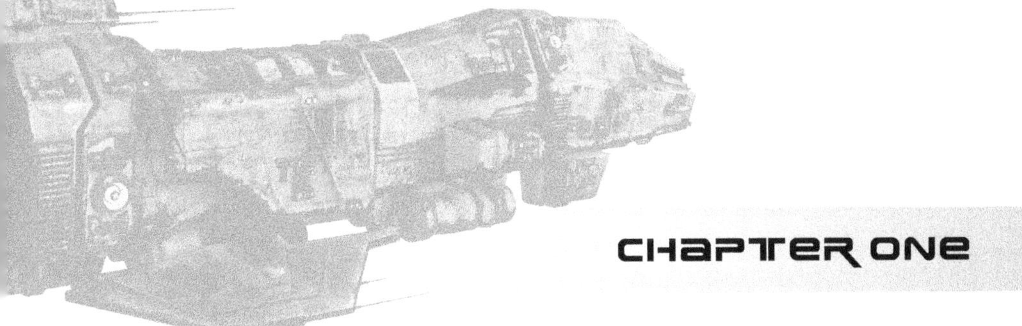

CHAPTER ONE

# CAN I GET HOME……? (IN MODERN DAY ENGLAND, UK)

Saturday morning was Steves favourite. This particular Saturday was bright and sunny. His local Coffee Shop was going to be his destination once again as "the Lads" would be there and Steve2 owed him £50 so he was on a winner today. He was running a bit late and parking was the usual problem; he had to drive a fair distance away and street park on the Council Estate that technically was for Residents only. Nobody knew he was not a Guest Visitor so he would again get away with it (hopefully and especially as he had mocked up a forged Annual PASS half hidden in his windscreen so a Parking Warden could not take incriminating details).

Steve had beaten the system for years now and bragged about this skill-set to all and sundry; anyone who would listen found out about his methods and why he was now a Local Hero. Residents hated all the Local Authority RULES and RESTRICTIONS increasingly being brought in and it was the number one topic of conversation at any open microphone Public Meeting nowadays.

Steve walked into the Coffee Shop and ordered his usual Decaf Latte and went to meet his friends. They were in fine form and before long it was his "round" so he ordered six drinks but he had got his £50 loan back from Steve2 so he took the hit with a smile.

As they were sipping coffee they noticed a rare event, no traffic along the one-way street outside the Coffee Shop. Bob got up and went outside to investigate (nobody else was that keen). When he returned, he told a staggering tale......

There was a bloody great articulated Lorry broken down and blocking the entire commercial street. No traffic could enter and use the town commercial centre and its one-way road system. It seemed the vehicle would need a bigger Lorry to rescue it by lifting or pulling it away. So much for the busiest day of the week when the most trading would be done. Shop-Keepers and Locals would be very angry!

Steve then thought he would return to his car and get his iPhone and take pictures as this was just awesome. When he got to his car, he saw he had a slow-puncture. He swore and cursed his luck before taking out the spare tyre which was obviously under-inflated but would be OK to get him home.

By the time he had the spare tyre fitted he was dirty and sweaty. When he returned to the Coffee Shop, he was the butt of all jokes. He did not see the funny side of things as he was worried about the spare tyre – would it stay inflated long enough for the road to clear so he could get out of Town (after the Lorry had been removed? No other route was possible.)

Down on his luck Steve sat in the Coffee Shop waiting for the Rescue Lorry. It got worse, Ginny arrived and asked for a lift home as she had an emergency and could he help? This was a miracle. He had been trying to impress her for months now and when she finally asks him, he cannot help. Was somebody up their trying to punish him? "*Sorry: no can do luv: Road is blocked so I can't use my car: otherwise I would have loved to of helped you: I have to wait here until the rescue Lorry backs in, if it can, and tows this wreck out.*"

His chance has gone.

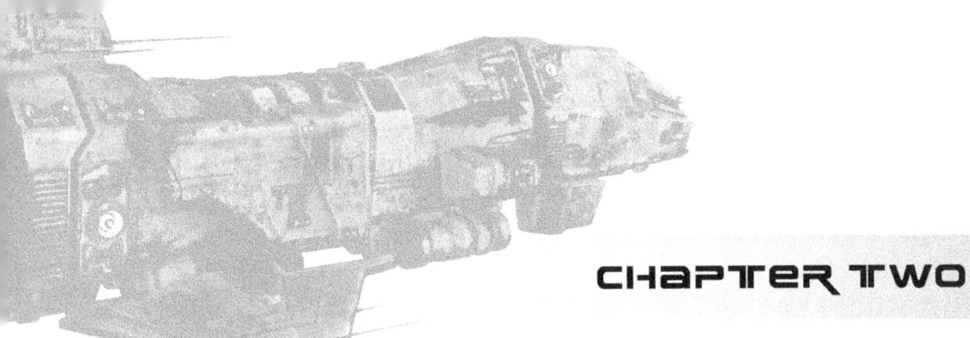

## CHAPTER TWO

# NOT HIS DAY!

STEVE *WHY ME? ALWAYS ME?*
An AVERAGE GUY.

As he moved his car a PARKING TICKET fluttered to the ground. He had been seen and ticketed by an observant Parking Warden. It had slipped from his windscreen wiper: how Steve had missed seeing it was anyone's guess. But surely it should have been stuck on???

What he should have also seen was a matchstick protruding from the spare tyre wheel valve and air was slowly hissing away; his wheel would be flat in perhaps another hours' time. The butt of some joker yet again!

As he left the **COFFEE SHOP,** he should have again also realised HE HAD NOT PAID for the round of coffees. How this would pan-out was also anyone's guess. Pay when he next enters (which was often), Police involved (probably not)?, stiff letter to him at home (they will know where he lives), etc..? Will he remember somewhen and call them to pay? Should they call him at home for payment? Could they forget to ask for payment as he was a good customer?

Steve returned to his car and saw the flat tyre. While investigating the tyre he also noticed the Parking Ticket on the ground closeby. He picked up the ticket through curiosity and immediately noticed it was for his car! His blood pressure rose several points (as did his swearing). Why me? It's always me; it's just not fair; they always pick on me! Bloody hell: hells bells! Sod it!............

He was naturally a loner; he could not match guys of his age bracket. Whether it be drink, sports, attracting the girls, things that money bought, the trappings of wealth. He knew he could never compete at that level. He just did not have the words nor the acting skills. Others might try it on and might even carry it off for a period but really sustain it and fool people long term? Real con-artists level? No, very few could do that and certainly not him.

Thoughts racing through his mind stopped Steve as he realised the time, he had promised his Mum he would be back for Lunch with her. *Dam, I had forgotten*! He turned and rushed back. He was pleased that his car had not been "lifted" or towed away so he just got in and drove off (after checking for wheel clamps).

So, this outing would cost him a Coffee round, the Tyre Repair plus a Parking Ticket: this was definitely not his day but would things get any better as the week gained momentum. He hoped so.

*"Another day another chance in life"* – was it his Grandfather who was always saying this, he could not remember. He would also say something like "*The* ***power to believe*** *was*

*important and so positive thinking was the order of the day/ week. A cheerful disposition was what was needed", and Steve added "but this was difficult under the circumstances".* His initial thought was usually to gauge the public position or tone: what were they thinking and what was their attitude to "life, the universe and everything"? Could he at least match that and then he would form an opinion or answer.

He had several friends that had this checked out and so had a reasonable idea of the tone of answer expected. That answer would be different to mine but such an answer (together with his wife's' – if he ever had one) would always been different to the rest of the worlds' as he was a self-proclaimed LONER with a small number of **lifelong good friends** and large number of ***acquaintance friends*** whereas his wife's profile was probably going to be in the opposite direction (he assumed). His best friend was going to be his future wife and he expected she would come from his past unless he got very lucky indeed. Since he was, say 12 years old, you could list him, Ginny, an old school chum

Dave, then this brother and wife (plus their two Children) to represent what he always called "his Family" or "The Family" and this made him feel warm and comfortable somehow.

As he was a calm/intelligent person, people often asked for his opinion of things: personal and business matters. He took this as a compliment but tried to avoid an extended answer if possible. They asked in the spirit of GOOD VIBRATIONS (Beach Boys song, October 1966, and England had just won the World Soccer Cup) but often what I had to tell them came under the category of BAD VIBRATIONS (ME, as a Book Author, and a retired House Surveyor, was well used to this scenario – this was why people commission private House Condition Surveys – to find out the truth which is sometimes hidden).

What life throws at you constantly challenges you either in a good way, but sometimes in a bad way. What counts is how you react and how you ultimately finish. ***Head Up,***

***Eye on the Ball, Keep Going*** is the attitude needed but do you have the stamina needed to achieve this. This is where friends and family come in- to help you play the long game of life. The short game has too many variables to control.

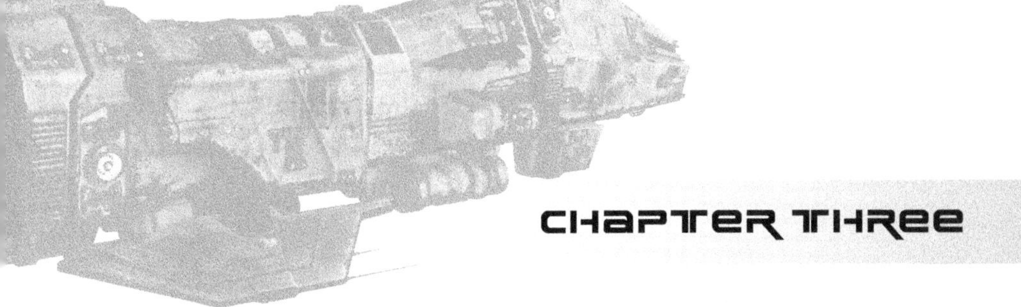

# CHAPTER THREE

## RESOLUTION

Steve wanted to impress Ginny: Ginny needed to go Home as her mother had called her as her grandfather had just suddenly (and unexpectedly) died. Her lovely, favourite Grandfather DEAD! Come home NOW, please.

Ginny and family were needed to deal with that crisis. However, she found it difficult to accept this as she had not yet accepted her favourite Family member had departed this worldly realm; how could he be gone as she had only had a great time with him yesterday and he was fine! Life was such a bitch at times. She reluctantly returned home and became tearful as she went through the back door and saw friends and family members beginning to express sympathy.

She had not experienced death before. She needed her mother to show her the required protocols and this annoyed her and made her feel useless initially. Once she realised that she was being stupid she calmed and came round to talking to relatives who seemed to appear from nowhere. Grandad was her "favourite," *he was not for anyone else*! The way some of her relatives and family friends were talking was unreal and annoying. She stomped off to her room for some peace and isolation.

Then the local Vicar appeared at Mums request. He was nice and he spoke about Personal Resolution and this made perfect sense to me but I could see Mum was bored. The Vicar went through the Service Order and asked if we had any special needs for the Service. Mum and daughter looked blank and basically took all the Vicars recommendations. Skip forward a few days and both are in a Church and the

Service had just finished. The congregation have left accept daughter and she begins to stare at the large silver Cross on the Alter and is transfixed. Apart from anybody who might be within the Vestry etc... She is alone and still I stare.

Suddenly she hears a voice, as if a shadow murmurs in the dark of night but somehow it is crystal clear: "***Ginny: I am with you and will not leave you: I have chosen you to spread my words. When appropriate I will make words depart from you when needed so have faith in me as it will be Jesus' speaking. Simply focus and ask for my help and it will be given. Have FAITH. It is as foretold.***"

The voice breaks off and it feels like she has just woken from a deep sleep but is now vibrant and ready for anything. However, she stops and intentionally stare at the silver cross which she removes and places in her rucksack (why, she unsure as it was a simple instinctive reaction).

She keeps asking herself questions like "Am I a Prophet now?" "Will they stone me – literally?". "Can I carry this off?". "Is this real or am I deluded?" "Am I to become another Jesus, direct from God?" "How the heck will this pan out?" "This is just unbelievable." "How will this end?" This is, or is this - the second coming as foretold?

The second coming in an age when we discuss sex, drugs, and rock-and-roll plus Alien Spacecraft in our atmosphere but also continuing war zones including fighting over religious stances. What have we learnt and where are we going? **We certainly need direction and advice.** Will we listen or are we deaf to reason? Has history taught us anything? Has wisdom ingrained itself in our consciousness so we can move forward or must we loop and therefore leap into fighting and starvation periods yet again. Watch this space.

This is important: Knowledge can be split into differing grades – one is a category that she calls "Outstandingly Amazing" (things we do not really need to know but when you do it blows your MIND) – let me illustrate:-

1. **The PACIFIC OCEAN is larger than all the LANDMASS of planet earth** — Pacific Ocean area extends to 165.25 million $km^2$ and the Earth landmass covers an area of 148.94 million $km^2$.
2. **All ROADS** (a very very large majority) do **actually lead towards ROME**. See Map attached
3. **Do you know** the difference between **GREAT BRITAIN** and the **UNITED KINGDOM.** Both include Scotland, England and Wales but only the UK also includes Northern Ireland. {Neither include the Isle of Man}.
4. **What are The SEVEN WONDERS of the ANCIENT WORLD?**

    1. Statute of ZEUS at Olympia
    2. Temple of Artemis at Ephesus
    3. Colossus of Rhodes
    4. Mausoleum at Halicarnassus
    5. Lighthouse of Alexandria

6. Hanging Gardens of Babylon (disputed)
7. Great Pyramid of Giza

Do you get my drift here?. The seven wonders of the world have been in existence for a long time: Rome and its roads actually do make sense but the scale of the roads is mind boggling. The GB/UK "difference" is a technicality which perhaps she never learned this at School.

Enough – So I appear to have become all powerful without anybody knowing or expecting it. **The VOICE has given me powers beyond belief** and I must accept this status and secondly understand the responsibility and thirdly try to enjoy this role. If needs be I could make time stand still so I can manipulate and "walk on". Does anyone really want the **almighty status** with people **bowing to you** and giving you **superstar acknowledgement all the time**. Perhaps me living in a mansion at the top of a hill with acres of grounds and having everything you ever dreamed of?

In today's timeframe too many people chase the dollar thinking that money changes everything: they are deluded. It is what people do with their money that changes things and they have no idea. House, Cars, Holidays, Clothes, Trinkets seems to be the template nowadays rather than helping others in the family and set up pension-funds, health-care reserves and finally perhaps charity to known specific persons to help others (strangers) as well your own community.

**Isn't life about personal achievements and striving for things. Surely also having relationships with other people is an equal so you are sharing and giving at the same time**.

Your **personal RESOLUTION** must be achieved so you know **HOW TO LIVE** a daily life so when your time is up you can look GOD and JESUS in the eye and say "**I did my best for one and all**". This is a personal and simple contract with the almighty which most have forgotten.

Surely it does not take much to understand this? Humans seem to try to make it more complex when simple language and actions are all that are needed. Jesus understood this but even his gentle ways could not penetrate the evil that protected the hard wickedness of an evil regime that felt threatened by his (Jesus) simple status and reputation. For this he paid the ultimate price.

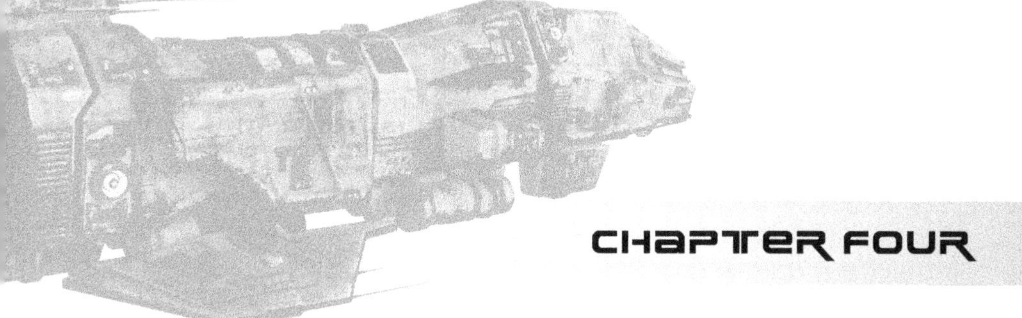

# CHAPTER FOUR

## GINNY & BEETHOVEN'S 5TH

Ginny had noticed that Steve had eyes for her. She was interested in him but he needed to come out of his shell and let his hair down. If only he would …… Others were closing in and she was only human and she had needs of her own and …….

Her phone chimed and she knew it was "him": she had programmed the iPhone just for this purpose and this was the first time Beethoven's 5th symphony had actually played indicating his incoming call! She smiled as the memory flashed across her mind {Steves House number 1808 and Beethoven finished writing this particular music in 1808:

*she liked details like this as it cemented her mind and perhaps, in her dreams, meant the two of them were fated to be together, a pair, a couple, one day?}.*

Hi Steve: Nice to hear from you.

Hi Ginny: I was wondering if I could buy you lunch at the pub today? How about it? Say half 12?

Steve had never been this bold and Ginny was amazed: she detected a trace of breath in the background and wondered if a "friend" was with Steve preverbally holding his hand to give him courage to phone her?

"Yes: thanks, I'll be there and will look forward to seeing you. I must go now as I am late for an Appointment." Bye. He reluctantly closed off the call and punched the air and shouted, YES YES!

The anticipation killed the day for Steve. He had periods of sweating and it seemed he could not keep still for more than five consecutive minutes; nervousness was eating into him as the day passed. Nevertheless 12:30 came and he found himself at the Pub and within just a couple of minutes his prize arrived. She had put her hair up and she looked drop-dead gorgeous in her plain jeans and small T-shirt that emphasised her fulsome figure.

Steve told himself to grow up as she made a bee-line for him. He rose to pull a chair out for her to sit. He knew his manners. He asked if she wanted her usual favourite drink or the Wine List? As he ordered he asked for both the Food and Wine Lists. They ended up just having Specials from the chalk Board plus usual drinks so no “Lists” were needed (much to his relief).

His fear rapidity dissipated as they both relaxed over Dish-of-the-Day, Meat Pie and Chips and their favourite tipples. Keep it Simple always works! Conversation was about friends and local issues plus a few minor scandals and, of course the recent case of the notorious Mr Wilson sent under for 10 years for roughing up and inflicting sexual acts upon Mary Gainsworth (who "had a history as long as......"). Most Villages have one such as him (and her?).

Steve had his first official lady friend and he was on top of the world. It just could not get any better than this.

CHAPTER FIVE

# FAIRGROUND & FAIRNESS?

By Ancient Charter Travelling Fun Fairs have a right to annually set up at certain places around the UK (eg: my local one is Wickham in southern Hampshire). As time has passed each STALL has grown and its owner has modernised such that it comes with perhaps one or more cars/vans (or a small Lorry) plus an Owners Caravan or even a large Mobile Home or two. Some of the Attractions are LARGE and WEIGHTY and require extensive electrical systems.

These events are great fun for the family. **But….**

A downside exists and I have experienced it. It revolves around "where do all the Vehicles and Cabins park/locate for the period of the event (one or two days BEFORE, the period of the event, the dismantle period + leaving day = several days). They need services – water, electricity and preferably sanitation.

Shops in the commercial Centre of the event close-down usually for ONE DAY and Car Parks become full long before the event. Therefore, Public Playing Fields are used for overfill Car Parks. Often Public Roads are closed and AA signs redirect or control traffic accordingly. A great deal of inconvenience.

- Extra Police patrols arranged and better general security is needed.
- Mobile Toilets are often arranged to stop public urination.
- Extra, mobile Street lighting may be required.
- Voluntary Medics may be required.
- Health & Safety certification will be needed.
- The whole area needs sanitation/cleansing afterwards.

The whole event becomes disproportionate to the gain by the Public. All a bit seedy. Street crime seems to get worse each year and perhaps takings are in a downward trend? I have not attended for perhaps 10/15 years and therefore cannot judge but hear all sorts of stories in that direction but do not know the actual facts. Am I getting Old and intolerant as the kid in me departs? No, I have a good sense of humour and like games of sport and chance. Perhaps I just crave something a little more sophisticated and not all things rough-and-ready or here-today-gone-tomorrow?

Reluctantly however I must balance my statements and say I would rather have the Fun Fair than see it fall away and become just a part of History. England is full of Traditions and History without which it would be a duller place.

Just like Steve. He would have been a good friend of mine as he verges on free-thinking and perhaps that is my own ace-or-trump-card?

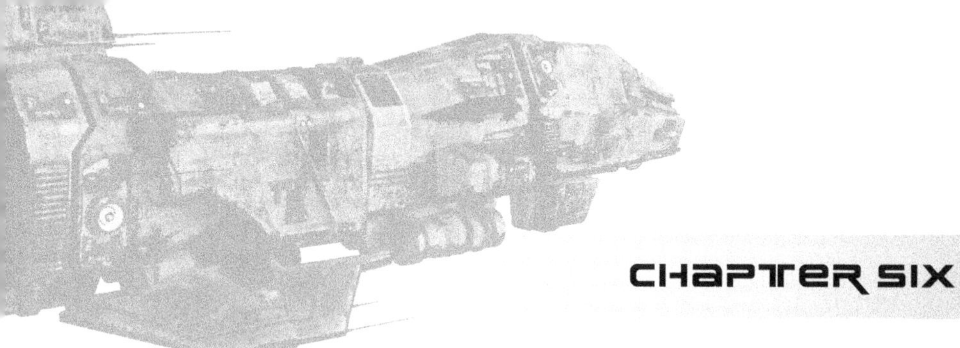

CHAPTER SIX

# BACK TO STEVE AND GINNY

The great reconciliation appears to be happening between them. Not only are they friends but a relationship is about to bloom. They spend large amounts of time together: they always seem to know what each other is about to say: they walk together: they do everything together: eye contact is far in excess of normal friendship levels: Steve has stopped asking for "group" opinion or answers, ONLY "her" answers to questions/riddles: everyone knows what is going to happen next……

Yes, they are holding hands, even kissing when they thought nobody was looking or could see them. Indeed, it was an open secret they may be lovers (well, maybe as that was so out of Steves character but he did have a certain sparkle in his eyes!).

**Hold the front page**! Steve and Ginny were seen coming out of Sunday Church and with Steves Mum. Now that is something that knocked the spots off everything you could think of. "No way" was the common reply as this news was circulated around town and beyond.

In fact, what they had seen was orchestrated by Steves Mum as she knew what was about to happen. She was not a mind-reader with special powers but had found an engagement ring in Steves Room and had demanded to know the score. Reluctantly Steve had confessed he was going to pop the question soon; much to his Mums delight.

Everyone was on Cloud Nine and this was in many ways hindering Steve as he wanted things to settle before he popped the question to Ginny. So, he waited. And waited. And waited. In fact, a further month went by much to his mum's annoyance. Others in the know were equally annoyed and the risk of somebody saying something "out of place" and "letting the Cat Out of the Bag" was getting higher and higher.

Steve realised he had to pop the question very soon and the Devil in him (yes, you heard me) thought of all sorts of scenarios that might work. But was Steve up to acting any scenario? Not really. His Mum settled it and told him to "*Man Up and do the decent thing. Ginny's Grandfather, God bless his departed soul, would have been shouting at you by now as he was as straight as could be and always did the decent and direct thing* (or words to that effect) *and especially as he was a good Christian.*"

Obviously, Steve must have done exactly this, or some such version. Good man!

This is where life gets very complex - - - - - - - - - - - - - -

**Ginny experienced the strangest event humankind ever wanted to see/hear but nobody else was exposed to her feelings and bliss....... except one man...... Steve.......**

It started with Ginny by the Town Lake watching Ducks and Birds feeding. She then realised that it was all (the world and everything) far too quiet and still. Then she leapt to her feet as the ducks and birds (yes, the birds in the air that were flying) just stopped in flight as if frozen in motion. She stood and turned and one-by-one noticed the details: the whole world had stopped. Completely. Totally.

Nothing was moving. This included the clouds and birds in the sky: the people, cars, and aircraft that she could see and all the people in her sight. Everything that could move was still, except HER.

The river was not frozen but just still as if frozen and she could see fish, also still.

She was trembling with fright now as she walked to her car (Mum had let her borrow it) but it would not work/ start. This confirmed that as far as she could detect/see SHE was the only thing that was moving or moveable in any line-of-sight. This confirmation made her fear transfer to a feeling of sickness more than fear. As far as she was aware SHE WAS THE ONLY THING UNAFFECTED AND MOVING.

At Home Ginny checked the TV and Radio – all dead. If this trend continued, she suspected Services would ultimately fail also. She was realistic and her thinking went "*If this continued dead bodies would decay; food would run out unless I hoard and freeze large amounts and start growing seasonal things* etc.... Then she froze and berated herself for starting to say such things. Freezing might not be possible?

The doorbell chimed: It was Steve: *"Come in. Thank goodness. What the hell is happening?"* This is surreal. Both had realised they needed each other and perhaps should join forces and prepare for the worse. Were they the only people left MOVING on earth? What was happening?

Does ***love conquer all*** after all?

CHAPTER SEVEN

# BACK TO STEVE AND GINNY, AGAIN!

Steve and Ginny were alive and living in the empty house in a street parallel to his Mums Home. It was one month since the Earth and people became frozen in every way, including time. Nothing moved. Why? They had no idea. The one thing they had noticed was that nothing decayed so food was not a problem which was their number one worry initially. Number two was water treatment Works would have stopped processing pure-flows and so safe drinking water could become a problem very soon. Steve was forever practical!

Ginny had declared that the two of them should consider themselves MARRIED. NO was the reply but instead they went to the Town Church in their best clothes and recited the marriage service in front of God at the alter and made their vows accordingly. They found a Marriage Register Book in the Vestry and filled in their names and the date plus a series of XXXX's for Witnesses etc.... This satisfied them and perhaps also God, to whom they spoke. Now they considered themselves married as witnessed by the ring.

They entered **a new world together** and wanted to travel to hopefully help others if possible (if they existed). So started their journeying.

Was this Gods Judgement (or Vengeance?) – **if you are free of sin,** you would be unaffected and would live a normal life and would not see a "frozen world – Earth1" but instead a vibrant, active loving world (Earth2 – perhaps?).

Was all this a part of a bigger plan? Were Steve and Ginny being released to spread the word of God in order the restart humanity? Two pilgrims to restart the world? This seemed somehow familiar. Pilgrims go forth (and multiple?). **Surely this meant others may exist.**

**Such was the power and wisdom of God. His watch was ticking if we did but know it. We thought his offspring was male but was instead a daughter whom we crucified. Post her resurrection - was our chance to reset that mistake and much later this gave us the chance that was DELIVERED by mild mannered Steve and beautiful Ginny (self-married in front of God) to reset the world.**

Steve and Ginny were given the understanding that they were special and were Pilgrims or even perhaps Disciples as they had an inner feeling of direction straight from God. No written contract or face-to-face instruction. More an inner understanding.

Steve now remembered his vision with Jesus/God. He settled himself and asked Ginny not to disturb him. He formed words in his mind. *God/Jesus be praised and hear my prayer:-*

*You told me to ask for help: here I am and I need to reaffirm my planning goals and what I need to bolster my chances of helping you and all the souls who need you:-*

- *Help me stand firm in the hour when I am provoked and set upon.*
- *Help me set a ridged and loud/strong example when tested by my enemies and avoid them if possible.*
- *Help me if I am tested by my enemies so I can save lives through wisdom.*
- *Help me protect your daughter wherever possible.*

**God replied** *that Steve was a Master Tactician and would help himself if his planning was thorough and thoughtful and based on good, up-to-date intelligence and was always needful.*

Those who plan well and in advance tend to not get picked on and it seemed society here had learned that lesson. Steve and Ginny were elevated from Provincial Town ordinary citizens up to World Leader category types within just months.

Steve had assumed the persona of a latter-day Saint spreading the word of God. Ginny was even more remarkable doing the same but to floods of women wherever she went. Yes, she eclipsed Steve as they had surmised: she was an Angel in their eyes. God simply smiled at them both and this was plain for all to see as their value grew and grew. They positively glowed – they had an aura like never before: they glowed with positivity and this spread to others when they preached. It was contagious. It was marvellous. It was a miracle in itself. They made everyone Smile!

CHAPTER EIGHT

# PLANNING & ANSWERS AT LAST

Steve and Ginny were brilliant in South Hampshire when Aliens had been discovered a few years ago. Another audience opportunity during another day?

Straight back to London with infrastructure to keep travelling alive and improve safety (they were always followed) yet still only a relatively short trip back home to the south coast.

This drove the march for greater involvement with Government and the local, southern, Authorities. That lesson had been obvious at the time and was even more important now. The importance of Water had also been learnt and we were under a duty to defend it by any legal means possible.

Satellite watch had been disabled so 24/7 direct visual watches had been set up now that The Solent was but River Scale/Width since the Grand Theft of Water by Aliens. Riverboat armament was limited so traps and alarms had been set up to warn of Tornado Attack (limited means of defence available against such strong vortex forces).

Steve had a bandwagon agenda of *"all forces should join together to increase strength rather than suffer the effects of disjointed power, management and timing/decisions". But does anybody even listen anymore*?". Too many conflicts of opinion/power. Too much to lose or gain?

Aliens were still on earth but had, as they had promised, rebuilt just about all the damage that fighting had caused so had had a net positive effect upon transport, markets, agriculture, machine/processing, computers, space travel/

engine design, biology, and a lot more: despite just about being a goldless planet.

Indeed, Aliens were offering a service that meant Earthling Families could be transported to a far, far away planet, like Earth but which required resettling to stabilise it. Ten of thousands had said YES to ease the beginnings of overcrowding issues here. Thank goodness. The outward trip would take about six months and so deep sleep was an option but most said no to this (probably out of mistrust and fear) rather than as a method of protecting their bodies.

Let's summarise:-

Earth was perhaps at its zenith and near to capacity population bearing in mind its climate and resources. We had been visited by Aliens so knew we were not alone in the big wide yonder and predictions were largely positive about our future assuming no mighty changes were enforced upon us or were needed for whatever reason. This seemed like good news to us.

This mindset was bolstered when Jesus returned in the form of Steve and Ginny touring the globe and seemingly being able to work miracles in the name of God Almighty through the spirit of Jesus. As the world was generally "doing well" was this then the **NEXT COMING**. Media had this question phrased as **"He can perform miracles, we have witnessed this, so why is he touring as he can reach trillions on Radio and TV"?**

Good question. Why? ***Personal witnessing (first hand evidence) has no substitute as it is a personal bonding experience unless you are prepared to let Pure Faith guide you*** is the only answer that Steve had given to any who asked this of him. Ginny had shortened this to "***Let your faith guide you.***"

***"If you only believe by SEEING IS BELIEVING then we will fail in our mission. Let your faith guide you".*** This was the core message being delivered by them. They told of the vibrant energy in their own souls and the way God had guided them to this place and has spoken to them and reassured them.

Indeed, God had spoked to them such that they could truly tell the world – "***You have heard the word of God delivered and so you know how to proceed. Do not let fear stop you as to have nothing to prevent you entering a better place***".

So, all Steve and Ginny needed was a status quo of:-

1. The Media to shout out that Steve and Ginny were available **for ALL TO ATTEND THEM**
2. To **HEAR the WORDS of GOD**
3. BUT – First **REPENT of your SINS**
4. You will then see a **BETTER WAY FORWARD**
5. RECEIVE a **TEMPLATE for PERSONAL ADVANCEMENT** as SPOKEN BY JESUS

**You have NOTHING to lose.**

COME.

CHAPTER NINE

# EXPLANATIONS MOVING FORWARD

Unexpectedly television came to Steve and Ginny's help one day. They were being interviewed by a famous Interviewer in a TV Centre Studio when the Interviewer mentioned her mother had cancer.

Ginny immediately stopped her in mid-sentence and said "No she has not got cancer; she is free of all disease and is well."

Pardon. What did you say? Ginny repeated herself. The Studio audience hushed. "***She is well and free of all contagion because I believe it,***" said Ginny. The lady Interviewer immediately pulled out her mobile phone and rang Mum. Mum was crying with joy as she was feeling calm and vibrant. She did not know what had happened but she said she suddenly felt fine and wholesome like a 20-year-old and she was going to go for a walk!

The audience exploded into cheering assuming all was well. It certainly seemed that way. The Interviewer called a recess of 30 minutes.

Backstage all hell was let loose. They had recorded a miracle (well, the daughters' reactions): close-ups of facial expressions, a casual flick of a hand or fingers, etc..... This was a first in many respects. This was a modern "laying on of hands" or "anointing with oils" or "reciting from Holy Books" etc..... Ginny and this footage would be analysed for years to come once the condition of the Interviewers Mother was verified as cancer free which all assumed for now (later this was verified).

Steve, not jealous but getting rather tired of all the chatter and fuss, suggested to Ginny that they made an exit sooner rather than later. Ginny agreed so they gave their thanks and made for the exits. Unfortunately, they were now superstars and they were mobbed mainly by the younger age-groups and it took thirty minutes just to get to their car that was within sight!

Tired, weary, and approaching annoyance they both retreated to Steves place to get something to eat and drink and did not want any visitors. A Whiteboard in a bedroom Office had produced a jazzy message that Steve liked – the message said:-

> **We are instruments of JESUS**: GOD asked us to show you **what FAITH can do** and **WE RESPONDED** to his **INVITATION**. Give **PRAISE TO THE ALMIGHTY** NOW.

He hoped the experience today would become commonplace within his daily life with Ginny. Batman and Robin updated to read **Steve & Ginny who can pack a punch**.

Indeed, today's experience was a benchmark for Ginny who later that evening expressed her feelings to Steve. If they needed to travel to spread the words of God/Jesus then so be it but let us get away from this Town, the place of our births. We need to upscale and explore this planet of ours and build our creditability.

And so, it had begun. They were not a Fairground Attraction but the beginning of the latest coming of the Divine Presence of Almighty God.

CHAPTER TEN

# THE UNEXPECTED

No sooner had things settled than we got the absurd:-

American, Houston Airbase Control Centre intercepted an Alien Craft headed for Earth. Needless to say, Planes went to guide it in and land with it for security purposes etc.... This was normal to staff at this Base, and this shook our intrepid duo and that told a story in itself. News of the landing was soon all around the planet. The Martians (or whoever they were) opened the entrance ramp of their Craft and began walking away as indicated by the massive 6ft 6ins military Trooper Guards with guns primed and ready to shoot. It was all a bit of an anticlimax now knowing this was "normal" and happened regularly (but was not reported to the masses).

It transpired the Aliens had pre-communicated a message to Earth that one of our returning unmanned Satellites had been contaminated with spores from a highly virulent virus that could do untold damage on earth if we did not immediately decontaminate it RIGHT NOW.

ALSO, Re-entry burnout would not be sufficient nor would washing by ocean landing. Aliens were saying decontaminate whilst in deep-space would be best so the ozone layers are not affected. They assumed we had craft ready to launch NOW to stop in the outer ozone layers and be capable of "catching and decomtaminating" both Craft and Bug Germs.

NASA had not given approval for such actions but did not pass this detail on to these Aliens. They considered burnout would suffice AND they would do special decontam actions in the ocean on Earth after placing the capsule within a special sealable cannister. **Thanks Aliens you can go now!**

Now, Aliens had intervened several times when big decisions had to be made over the years. This would be the ninth time, not that this data was ever released to the public. Our history of accepting or taking advice given was not high and why should it be as we have no way to gauge its accuracy other than "the eventual outcome" (which was always good – as measured by hindsight/time).

Needless the say this so-call superbug hit earth badly as it made humans unable to assimilate oxygen and so death came calling quickly. Once dead each corpse magnified the bug spores and so the outbreak grew quickly and geographically unless extremely well contained. This was a global pandemic waiting to happen. A true nightmare, class one.

However, for once lady luck turned her face towards America and NASA. The Global tour of Steve and Ginny had detoured to NASA as Steve could not resist the chance to see *Real Rockets*. Whilst on-site they were grabbed and once the dilemma was explained they stepped up to the plate and cured the problem easily. Solved by a healing touch of magic from the English for a change but their legacy would run forever (they hoped).

One day Steve was stopped in his tracks but an innocent bystander who simply asked "*Why the headphones*?" (it was surprising nobody had queried this before). Steve gave a simple reply that he had his current favourite tune on a looped playlist as music was core to keeping him calm and able to work well. The back-up question was "*What tune is currently playing*?" to which the answer was *"Maxwell's Silver Hammer" by Brad Mehidau (a "live" version).*

This exchange seemed to humanise Steve and made the national Newscasts that day. The ***Power of Music*** as one Network put phrased it. It also did sales for Brads music a lot of good!

CHAPTER ELEVEN

# ACHIEVING A STARTING POINT

World population now had to assimilate all this data and decide how to accept/decline/react to it as it rippled piecemeal from continent to continent, home to home, family to family, man to woman, son to daughter. You had two miracle workers touring your planet aligning themselves with Jesus of Nazareth performing real miracles in the name of God Almighty. They were in their 20's and may continue for a lifetime so this was a long-term scenario.

You would not gain any merit points for guessing that much difference of opinion was being kicked around. From entrenched viewpoints of the traditionalists right through to the avant-garde youngsters with an eye for change in everything perhaps just for the sake of newness and doing away with the old.

Perhaps my view was that we had a new asset, Steve and Ginny, never seen before that was so massive and without comparison, that big changes had to be made to accommodate them. Simple yet massive in scope and benefit yet many people would be ejected in their wake (which was sad). I think this made me a modernist behind Steve and Ginny as leaders in this new **SALVATION FOR SINLESS PEOPLE MOVEMENT.** Its size would gain momentum by the good it achieves. They must demonstrate their worth continually to prove they were not fraudsters.

So, we had a **starting point**: what was needed was a **set of rules** for people to work with, to aspire to, to pledge knowledge of, etc....

We took many weeks to agree this list as it needed to be short and snappy and those that matter just could not agree so finally Steve and Ginny "had the final say." They "agreed" a short listing of:- Before I list anything let's be clear that they basically produced of the beginnings of the American Constitution (from memory and that was quite a feat):-

- Establish Justice
- Insure domestic Calm
- Provide for the common Defence
- Promote general Welfare
- Secure the Blessings of Liberty to ourselves and our Prosperity, to ordain and establish this Constitution….

These were a working draft and were simple and they seemed to not be contentious. So, Job done. I think the rest is history. The Movement sky-rocketed such that it is not really a Movement any more. The world population simply read the five core Banners/Words and invited Steve and Ginny to massive Gatherings on all the Continents. The world wanted them and they responded positively.

# S&G

"**S&G**," as they have affectionately become (a brand), are the prime guest speakers everywhere and occasionally they performed miracles (in emergencies), but never "on demand." The miracle is really in spreading the word of God and bringing comfort to those in need. They slammed any effort to make their message(s) any different back into the faces of any who went off their stated course.

When people asked for justifications, they simply said it was ***Gods will: have faith child!*** *(rightly or wrongly, we were at the stage that they felt they did not have to continually prove themselves. You bought into their standards and loving lifestyle or you did not; the choice was yours and always had been. Do not blame others. God Guides, God Loves, God will Reward You in* Heaven if you can truly **Believe** *and live a clean lifestyle.*

**Get to this point** and your life will change beyond recognition: start by truly repenting of your sins and then following the Ten Commandments and follow the S&G life pattern as being circulated.

***Respect all life*** became the buzz phrase to kick start a new initiative to get people to think more deeply about what surrounds their lifestyle and how they should attempt to build FAITH into their lives. Anticipation and Expectation rose and SMILES were everywhere were the result as the sense in "all this" was seen and the result very soon came filtering through all around. **People felt great**: uplifted seemed inadequate as they struggled to find the right words and burst out laughing with delight and told magnificent stories of what they expressed as their conversion to a better lifestyle.

But what they did was mostly ALL BY THEMSELVES. When they realised this they cried, laughed or were just astounded but best of all they SMILED.

Many noticed this and SMILING characterised the end result of the people realising they had chained themselves to endless boredom by simply not enjoying life. For example, going to the market to buy food was once a costly negative but now it was a chance to see friends and perhaps get a bargain having broken the boredom of the weeks' rhythm. It is what you make it, NOT what it makes you.

Was this a miracle OR Life just working itself out? The latter, and note that life produces miracles all around us every day and we do not even notice them as we are so wrapped up in our own lives and just do not care anymore about others' problems and successes. Open your eyes for once and CARE!

STEVE BEFORE CONVERSION

This is why this Chapter is titled "**ACHIEVING A STARTING POINT**" as we all need to reassess our core values and the way we interact with those all around us, 24/7. Neighbours, on the Bus/Train, at Work, at

Sporting Events etc.... And especially in how we bring up (and train) our Children. Do not let them be afraid of strangers so create a safe environment for kids to meet strangers (obviously highly important and they must be taught how to know what signs indicate the various levels of danger as we are all under a duty to operate common-sense EG: When not to meet Strangers).

And who brings up our Children? Obviously, its starts with women (birth) but from then on it is a shared responsibility with the actual split decided between the man/woman (in natural relationships) by agreement depending on individual personal circumstances/attitudes and family circumstances.

Achieving the **STARTING POINT marks the END of this SHORT STORY.** Women create the circle of life as surely as "all roads lead to Rome" but the journey is a joint venture. Yes, exceptions exist but in the main life is determined by general flows and those have been determined by women, in the main, although moulded slightly by men. This is how it should be. Life is a series of educated compromises. Jesus came and reminded us of this in his/her simple lifestyle and works.

Milton Keynes UK
Ingram Content Group UK Ltd.
UKHW011124170624
444031UK00018B/22